DOORWAY TO THE WORLD

DOORWAY TO THE WORLD

Written by
RONALD KIDD

Illustrated by
TERESA FLAVIN

A Habitat for Humanity Book

HABITAT FOR HUMANITY INTERNATIONAL
Americus, Georgia

In memory of Minnie Porter
—R.K.

To P.R.
—T.F.

Published by Habitat for Humanity International
121 Habitat Street
Americus, Georgia 31709-3498
1-800-422-4828

Millard Fuller   *President and Founder*
Joy Highnote   *Director, Product Development*
Joseph Matthews   *Director, Communication Services*

Edited, designed, and manufactured by
The Children's Marketplace
A division of Southwestern/Great American, Inc.
2451 Atrium Way, Nashville, Tennessee 37214
1-800-358-0560

Dave Kempf   *Vice President, Executive Editor*
Mary Cummings   *Managing Editor*
Ronald Kidd   *Project Editor*
Bruce Gore   *Book Design*

Text copyright ©1996 by Habitat for Humanity International
Illustrations ©1996 by Teresa Flavin

ISBN 1-887921-25-7
Library of Congress Catalog Number 96-077091

Their sound has gone out to all the earth,
and their words to the ends of the world.

Romans 10:18

It was a nice old house, but the door was what made it special.

The door was made of oak, with a brass handle and hinges. It was smooth to the touch and seemed to glow in the morning sun. The door was heavy, but it was so well made that it glided open with a just a click and a whisper.

Ben knew all about the door, because he had helped his mom and dad work on it when they first moved in. They sanded it to take away the rough places. They put on a coat of varnish, to make it gleam. They polished the handle and oiled the hinges.

As soon as the door was finished, people
began knocking on it. Neighbors came from
up and down the block to see who was living
in the old house. They brought cookies and
candy and homemade pies.

When they found Ben's family fixing up the place, the neighbors offered to help. It seemed as if every time the door opened, Ben and his parents made more friends. Family and friends worked side by side, and soon the old house looked like new.

But the workers didn't stop there. They knew there were other families in town whose houses could not be fixed. And so they joined a group called Habitat for Humanity.

Habitat for Humanity selects working families in need and helps them build clean, decent housing. The families work with Habitat volunteers, such as Ben's parents and friends. The volunteers don't get paid. They work because they want to help.

One day, after Ben had been living in his house for a long time, there came a knock at the door. It was a woman from Habitat for Humanity. She told Ben's parents that they had been picked by Habitat to be International Partners. She smiled and gave them a hug. She even kissed Ben on the cheek.

After the woman left, Ben's mom and dad danced across the floor. They joined hands with Ben, whirling around and around the room. When they finished, Ben asked what an International Partner was.

Ben's parents explained that International Partners are volunteers who are trained and sent by Habitat to other countries. They usually stay for three years, learning the language, living with the people, and helping them build houses.

Ben wasn't sure he liked the idea. How
could he leave his town? What about all his
friends? When Ben went to bed that night,
he locked the door and huddled under the
covers. Soon he fell into a restless sleep.

Deep in the night there was a noise.
Ben got up to look and was surprised to
find the door open. When he touched the
knob to close it, the door burst loose from
its hinges and circled the room. Before Ben
could say a word, the door swept him off
his feet and into the darkness.

Ben flew over the trees and across the mountains, until moonlight gave way to the sun. When he looked down, he found himself on the other side of the world.

Holding on tight, Ben watched in
wonder as he passed over country after
country, through wind, snow, sand, and
rain. Wherever he went, Habitat for
Humanity was at work, building houses.

In Uganda, workers made bricks out of
the red clay soil. The bricks were stacked
with mortar in between, to form sturdy
walls that would shut out the wind and sun.

In the Philippines, wooden houses were built on a foundation of concrete blocks, to prevent flooding from heavy rains. Proud new homeowners were already planting vegetable gardens and rows of colorful flowers.

In Guatemala, houses were made of
concrete blocks with steel bars, to help
them resist damage from earthquakes.

In each country there were people who looked different and spoke a different language. But all of them had one thing in common. With the help of Habitat for Humanity, they were building houses. And International Partners led the way.

The door banked to the left and headed
home. Sometime between sunset and dawn
Ben found himself back in bed.

The next morning, Ben got up and hurried to the door. He was surprised to find that it looked the same as ever. There was no sign of rain or snow or sand.

Ben knew he must have been dreaming. But it was a good dream—a dream of a world very much like his town, where neighbors help each other, where friends come in different colors, and where, by working together, people can have decent houses in which to live.

When Ben's mom and dad joined him at the door, he told them he was ready to be an International Partner. He would miss his town and friends but knew they would be waiting for him when he returned.

Gazing through the open doorway at the rising sun, Ben watched the day begin and wondered what new adventures it would bring.

RONALD KIDD is the author of thirty books for young audiences and five plays. He received the Children's Choice Award and was nominated for the Edgar Allan Poe Award. Two of his plays were selected for development at the Eugene O'Neill Theater Center's National Playwrights Conference. He lives with his wife in Nashville, Tennessee.

TERESA FLAVIN, a native of New York state, studied illustration at Massachusetts College of Art and Syracuse University. She has contributed illustrations to several children's novels, anthologies, and educational materials. *Doorway to the World* is her first picture book. Teresa lives with her husband in Glasgow, Scotland.

Habitat for Humanity International
121 Habitat Street
Americus, Georgia 31709-3498

For more information, please call
1-800-HABITAT